Adapted by Justine Korman

Illustrated by Bill Langley and Ron Dias

A GOLDEN BOOK • NEW YORK

www.goldenbooks.com

www.randomhouse.com/kids/disney

Educators and Librarians, for a variety of teaching tools, visit us at www.randomhouse.com/teachers

Library of Congress Control Number: 90-084874

ISBN: 978-0-7364-2420-2

Printed in the United States of America 10

Pongo, Perdita, and their fifteen puppies lived in a cozy little house in London. Their humans lived there, too: Roger, who was tall and thin and played the piano, and Anita, who laughed a lot. They all got along splendidly and were very happy.

Then one day the doorbell rang, and in came Cruella De Vil, Anita's old friend from school.

"How marvelous!" Cruella said, stroking the puppies' soft fur. "I'll take them all. The whole litter."

"I'm afraid we can't give them up," gasped Anita. "Poor Perdita . . . she'd be heartbroken."

"Don't be ridiculous," said Cruella. "You can't possibly afford to keep them."

"We are not selling the puppies," replied Roger, "and that's final!"

Furious, Cruella stamped out of the house.

One frosty night a few weeks later, Pongo and Perdita went out for a walk with Roger and Anita. The puppies were at home, asleep in their basket.

Suddenly, two men burst into the house. They put all the puppies into a big bag. Then they carried the bag out to their truck and sped away.

After being in the truck for what seemed like hours, the fifteen puppies found themselves in a room filled with many other Dalmatian puppies. On a couch in front of a television set were the two nasty men who had kidnapped them.

The other Dalmatians told them that the men worked for Cruella De Vil, who had bought the puppies from pet stores.

Back at home, Pongo and Perdita were horrified to find their puppies missing.

Pongo heard Roger tell Anita he suspected Cruella De Vil had stolen the puppies.

"Perdy, I'm afraid it's all up to us," said Pongo. "There's the Twilight Bark." The Twilight Bark was a system of long and short barks used by dogs to pass along news.

The next evening, Pongo and Perdita went on another walk with Roger and Anita. While the Dalmatians were out, they barked long and loud. They wanted all the dogs in London to be on the lookout for their puppies.

Pongo waited for someone to answer his barks. It was a very cold night, and most dogs were inside. Then Perdita added her bark to Pongo's, and at last they heard a reply.

It came from a Great Dane, who relayed the message to every other dog within barking range.

That night, the Twilight Bark even reached a quiet farm, where an old sheepdog known as the Colonel lay sleeping.

"Colonel, sir!" shouted Sergeant Tibs, a cat who lived on the farm. He had to let the Colonel know about the vital message coming in.

The Colonel lifted one shaggy ear to listen to the faint message. "It's from London. Fifteen spotted puddles stolen. Of course—puppies!" he cried.

"Two nights past, I heard puppy barking," Tibs said, remembering as he pointed to the De Vil mansion.

The Colonel barked a message back to London. Then he told Tibs, "I suppose we'd better investigate!"

They headed straight for the gloomy De Vil mansion. Tibs held on tight to the Colonel's back as he rushed through the snow.

Once they arrived, Tibs climbed onto the Colonel's shoulders. He peeked through an open window.

"Psst! Are you one of the fifteen stolen puppies?" he asked a little puppy without a collar.

"They're over there," said the puppy.

The men heard the noise and went to investigate. Tibs and the Colonel ran away, but not before promising to get help.

The next morning, Cruella De Vil arrived.

"It's got to be done tonight!" she cried.

"You couldn't get a half dozen coats out of the whole caboodle," complained one of her men, pointing to the puppies.

"Then we'll settle for half a dozen," said Cruella, "but do it!"

She dashed out and roared off in her car.

Sergeant Tibs and the Colonel had returned just in time to hear Cruella give the order. "Hey, kids, you'd better get out of here if you want to save your skins," Tibs whispered. Then he shoved one of the puppies toward a hole in the wall.

One by one, the other puppies followed.

Suddenly, the two thugs realized that the puppies were escaping. The chase was on! Tibs and the puppies scooted through the dark halls of the mansion. Soon they found themselves trapped at a dead end. The thugs raised their clubs to strike.

At that moment, Pongo and Perdita crashed through the window with a blast of glass and freezing air. The angry Dalmatian parents fought off the surprised men as all the puppies scampered to safety.

Once the dogs were safely outside, they thanked the Colonel and Tibs and said good-bye. Then they hurried toward London. Pongo and Perdita led the way, their fifteen puppies and all the other Dalmatian pups right behind them.

When they reached a frozen stream, they carefully crossed the slippery surface so they wouldn't leave paw prints. Then they resumed the race home.

All along their route, the Dalmatians were helped by other dogs. A black Labrador retriever arranged for them to ride to London in a moving van. The Dalmatians waited in a shed while the van was being fixed.

Suddenly, Cruella's big car pulled up outside. Somehow she had followed their tracks.

"Pongo," said Perdita. "How will we get to the van?"

Pongo noticed lots of ashes in the fireplace. If they all rolled in the soot, they would look just like black Labradors.

When the van was ready, the dogs marched outside. One after another, the soot-covered puppies were lifted into the van. Before Pongo had a chance to pick up the last one, a clump of snow fell from the shed onto the puppy.

Pongo snatched up the pup, but the snow had washed away the soot. From her car, Cruella could see the white fur and black spots.

"There they go!" she shouted as the van pulled away.

Faster and faster went the van, but Cruella's car drew closer and closer. She was screaming in anger. Then she began to yell in fear. Her car skidded on the icy road. Cruella tried to stop it, but her car spun around and slid into a ditch.

The last the Dalmatians saw of Cruella, she was standing beside her wrecked car having a nasty temper tantrum.

When the van reached the cozy little house in London, Roger and Anita were overjoyed. And when they counted the dogs, they discovered that they now had one hundred and one Dalmatians!

"We'll buy a big place in the country," said Roger. "We'll have a Dalmatian plantation!"

And they did exactly that. Pongo, Perdita, and all the spotted puppies lived there happily ever after.